Christmas Puppy

Official Santa's Helper Certificate

My puppy's name is <u>ruffis</u>

Arrived on <u>Sep \ 19 \ 2018</u>

Signature: *Santa Claus*

FROM NORTH POLE
DELIVERY

Christmas Puppy

It's wintertime! It's snowing,
children laughing as they play
in great anticipation
of their very favorite day!

3

It's Christmastime, when big leaf piles
give way to snowy days.
The North Pole buzzes as the elves
prepare for holidays.

They're making toys, they're singing songs,
a smile on every face.
Christmas magic fills the air
within this happy place.

Santa Claus checks his lists
of children near and far.
He'll be bringing gifts to them,
no matter where they are.

But before he does his job,
there are some things he must know—
who's been naughty, who's been nice—
so off his helpers go!

Santa's helpers make their way
to every child's house.
They sneak in when you don't expect,
as quiet as a mouse.

So close your eyes and count to 10,
then look around and see
what Santa Claus has sent to you—
a cuddly puppy!

He's come along to be your friend
this happy time of year.
He loves to make you laugh and smile
and bring you Christmas cheer!

Your puppy found the perfect home,
but there's something you must do.
He needs a special, brand-new name—
the perfect one from you!

As all the gifts are being wrapped
and placed beneath the tree,
your puppy watches everything—
and you, especially!

He waits to see how nice you are
to family and friends.
Are you naughty? Are you nice?
And do you lend a hand?

HAPPY
HOLIDAYS!

Then at night, when you're in bed
and sleep has come your way,
he travels back to Santa
and tells about your day!

Then, just like that, when morning comes,
your pup is back with you
to play and snuggle and keep watch
of all you say and do.

He does this every single night.
He travels oh-so far
to give the news to Santa Claus
of just how good you are.

Then, finally, on Christmas Eve,
your puppy's job is done.
And now—oh, joy!—it's Santa's turn
to visit everyone!

So be good and kind toward others
and remind yourself each year:
the puppy that you're hugging
may be Santa's eyes and ears!

Written by Tammi Salzano
Illustrated by Gladys Jose

an imprint of

■SCHOLASTIC
www.scholastic.com

Published by Tangerine Press, an imprint of Scholastic Inc., 557 Broadway, New York, NY 10012

10 9 8 7 6 5 4 3 2 1

ISBN: 978-1-338-25643-7

Printed in Jiaxing, China
592571 06/18